Text copyright © Leon Garfield 1994
Illustrations copyright © Philip Hopman 1994

First published in Great Britain in 1994
by Simon & Schuster Young Books
Campus 400
Maylands Avenue
Hemel Hempstead
Herts HP2 7EZ

Typeset in 16/24pt Sabon by Goodfellow & Egan Ltd, Cambridge
Printed and bound in Portugal by Ediçoes ASA

British Library Cataloguing in Publication Data available.

ISBN 0 7500 1492 X
ISBN 0 7500 1493 8 (pb)

Leon Garfield

SABRE-TOOTH SANDWICH

Illustrated by Philip Hopman

SIMON & SCHUSTER
YOUNG BOOKS

Chapter One

The sun went down as red and angry as my father's face; and still no sign of my uncle.

"If anything's happened to him," my mother told my father, with tears in her eyes (for my uncle is her only brother and she loves him dearly), "I'll never forgive you!" And she picked up the old mammoth tusk she thumps meat with, to make it tender.

Not that we've had any meat for the past
four days, only roots and stinking fish. But
before I tell you why, I ought to explain that
we are a family of cave-dwellers: my father,
my mother, my five sisters, my uncle, and me.

We live, says my uncle, at the dawn of history, and are really quite primitive; which drives my father mad. "Speak for yourself!" he shouts, and reaches for his club.

"Don't you dare lay a finger on him!" cries my mother, and my father mutters under his breath that he had something more substantial than a finger in mind; and he scowls like a thunder-sky as my uncle warms himself at the fire he's never fed, and stuffs himself from the pot he's never filled.

My uncle is a neat little man, with silverish hair, a fine brow, a big nose, a tremendous voice; and, says my father, two left feet. There, and even my mother has to admit it, my father has a point. My uncle has never been a great success in life. The truth of the matter is, he is more of a thinker than a doer; he likes to sit by the fire, just thinking.

My father says he is a lazy, no-good layabout, and if he wasn't my mother's brother, he'd be out of our cave faster than smoke.

But whatever might be said against him, nobody can deny that my uncle is always very well turned-out. Just because we live at the dawn of history, he says, there's no need to go about looking as if we've just got out of bed. Which is all very well, says my father angrily, but clean toe-nails and a bearskin hat won't feed nine hungry mouths!

Chapter Two

Usually my uncle, who is the best-tempered man in the world, takes my father's remarks in good part. He smiles and nods as if he agrees with every word of them; but the other day – it was five days ago – my father said something that got under my uncle's skin. You could tell by the way he looked up, as if he'd sat on a sharp stone.

"If only," my father said to my mother, "he got his hands dirty once in a while, I'd have a little more respect for him."

Next morning, after my father had gone hunting, my uncle said he was going out. "Where to?" asked my mother; but he only smiled and tapped the side of his nose.

He was gone for about two hours. When he came back, his eyes were shining hugely. He'd found just the thing, he said, that would please my father enormously. He wanted me and my sisters to help him fetch it back.

It turned out to be a hollow tree-trunk, as smooth and pale as stone. It was exactly the right size and height, he explained, for my father to stand his spears in.

We brought it
back and stood it upright
beside the entrance to our cave.

My mother thought it looked very well; but
wouldn't it be better if my uncle cut off the
branch that was sticking out from the bottom?
No, said my uncle wisely, it was needed to
keep the trunk steady.

My father came home quite late. He'd killed a pig and was carrying it over his shoulder. "Dinner for nine!" he called out cheerfully; then he tripped over the branch and broke his toe.

Although nobody told my father that it had been my uncle's idea to leave the branch poking out across the entrance, somehow he seemed to know.

He told my mother that this time her brother had struck a blow, not only at him, but at the whole family. Until my father's toe was better, my uncle would have to go out hunting; and my mother knew what that would mean: we would all starve.

We finished off the pig that night, which was five days ago; and as my father prophesied, it was the last good meal we've had.

Every morning my uncle sets off into the forest, and every afternoon he comes back, worse than empty-handed. Already he's lost my father's best spear and the head off my mother's axe. This morning, he took my father's club.

"It's his last chance!" shouted my father, loudly enough for my uncle to hear. "If he doesn't come back with something for the pot, I'll put him in it, so help me, I will!"

Chapter Three

The last of the red had gone, and black dragons were sprawling across the sky. The forest was dark and quiet, like a huge ragged hole in the night, full of sharp death and, somewhere, my uncle.

We went down to the edge of the trees, and called, and shouted; but he never came, he never answered.

My mother blamed my father. My uncle must have taken my father's words too much to heart and had exposed himself to some terrible danger rather than come home without our dinner. "If anything's happened to him," wept my mother, "I'll never forgive you!"

Then, even as she spoke, there came a loud cry from outside. A moment later, a frantic creature staggered into our cave, gave another cry, and collapsed by the fire like a heap of leaves. It was my uncle.

He was a pitiable sight. His hair was wild, his clothing filthy, and his face and arms and legs all smeared with blood. But he was alive!

"Where's my club?" demanded my father, while my mother wiped my uncle's brow and picked the twigs from his hair.

My uncle stared at him as if he could scarcely believe it possible that my father should be so hard-hearted as to be more worried about his club than about my uncle's health. "Tiger," he murmured faintly. "Sabre-toothed tiger."

My father lost his temper. "I may be primitive," he shouted, "but I'm not stupid! There hasn't been a sabre-toothed tiger in these parts since your grandfather's day!" and he went on to tell my mother that, even though he was only a Stone Age man living at the dawn of history, he wasn't going to have his intelligence insulted by that idle parasite (he meant my uncle) painting himself all over with blackberry juice and saying he'd met a sabre-toothed tiger.

"If only," said my father, "he'd made a real effort to *make* me believe him, I'd have had a little more respect for him!"

My uncle sat up sharply. Once again, my father had said something that had got under my uncle's skin. He stood up and, waving aside my mother's efforts to stop him, he began to do some very strange things.

He stared round our cave. He frowned. He
went to the back and cleared away some skins
my sisters had been working on. He told me
and my sisters to move the hollow tree-trunk
to an exact spot he pointed out, while he
arranged the skins in a snaky line across one
corner.

This done, he stepped back and studied the effect from every part of the cave. "Yes," he murmured, "I think that will do." Then he picked up an axe handle and swung it vigorously two or three times in the air.

"Yes," he murmued again, "I think this will do."

Now he came to each of us in turn and, very quietly, told us what he wanted; and, although it was strangeness piled on top of strangeness, not even my father questioned him. Maybe it was because we were light-headed from hunger, or because we'd seen something in my uncle we'd never seen before – a lightness of step, an easiness, an air of authority – that his words filled us with a feeling of tremendous adventure.

Chapter Four

Everything was ready. My uncle clapped his hands. "Beginners, please!" At once, we moved to our appointed places, and my uncle went outside.

As we waited, watching the entrance of our cave, I began to feel afraid that I would do something wrong. I think we all must have felt the same. I could see my sisters trembling; and my father and mother were looking pale. Then my uncle came into the cave.

27

He came in very stealthily, half-crouching, and grasping our axe handle as if it was my father's club. He paused at every step, and peered cautiously about him. Once, his gaze fell on me; but he didn't see me. He was no longer in our cave; he was alone in the forest, and I was a bush. I didn't dare to move.

It was truly amazing. The walls of our cave
had vanished, and there was my uncle,
creeping among huge, shadowy trees, fighting
his way through tangled branches, and
running swiftly across the open glades.

Even the snaky line of skins had disappeared. In its place, most mysteriously, was a wandering forest stream. You could tell, because my uncle knelt down and drank from it.

He rose, wiped his lips, and, with a quick glance about him, crept on, deeper and deeper into the forest.

Suddenly he stopped. He was most
marvellously balanced on one foot, with the
other just raised behind him, and with one
hand outstretched. It was almost as if he was
going to fly. He was absolutely still, save for
his eyes. They turned, and glittered sharply.
He had seen our dinner!

A deer was drinking from the stream; a beautiful creature with enormous brown eyes, just like my mother's.

Slowly, slowly, my uncle began to advance, with club uplifted. You could see his lips moving: "Dinner for nine!"

But my uncle was not the only hunter in the
forest. Deep among the trees, glaring with
horrible eyes, was a monstrous sabre-toothed
tiger! Silently, and limping a little from a
broken toe, it crept forward and crouched
down behind a bush. I could hear its low
growl and feel its hot breath on the back of my
neck.

I've never been so frightened in all my life! I
longed to shout out to my uncle, "Look
behind you!" but I was only a bush. All I could
do was to shake and shiver as if a gale was
blowing through my leaves.

34

The deer looked up from the stream. I don't know if the shaking bush had disturbed her, or if she'd caught a whiff of sabre-toothed scent; but she was plainly uneasy. She saw my uncle; then she saw the tiger. Her beautiful eyes grew round with terror.

At once my uncle guessed, from her pitiful expression, that there was some terrible danger behind him. He turned. He saw the tiger making ready to spring. He looked back. He saw the deer's despair; and instead of flying for his life and leaving the helpless deer to be torn into pieces, he did the bravest thing I've ever seen. He rushed straight at the monster with nothing but his bare hands and our axe handle!

Of course, the sabre-toothed could have smashed my uncle with one blow of its paw; but it was distracted by the whirling club. It snarled and snapped and at last seized hold of it in its jaws.

Then the great beast howled in fury! The club was firmly wedged in between its enormous teeth! Frantically it rushed about, shaking its head, until the club struck against a hollow tree-trunk, with a loud thwack.

At once there was a furious buzzing. The tiger had dislodged a swarm of large bees! Enraged, they flew at the disturber of their peace. In an instant, the deer and my uncle were forgotten as the sabre-toothed tried to shake off the fiercely attacking bees.

"Quick, quick!" cried the deer, too excited to hold her tongue. "Onto my back and away!" And while the maddened tiger raged and roared, my uncle jumped onto my mother's back and the pair of them galloped tremendously away!

Chapter Five

We all burst out cheering! We couldn't help it.
We were all so happy that my uncle and the
deer had got away.

"But why," my father asked my mother
when my uncle had got off her back, "didn't
he bring the deer back for the pot?"

My mother looked at him as if he was the most primitive cave-dweller she'd ever laid eyes on. "Just because you are a Stone Age man," she told him, "you don't have to have a heart of stone as well! The deer saved his life."

My father scratched his head. He turned to my uncle. "And did it really happen like that?"

My uncle looked him straight in the eye. "You saw for yourself, didn't you?" he said.

But that wasn't the end of it; the best was still to come. It turned out that some of our neighbours had been watching, from the entrance to our cave. They were amazed. They couldn't believe what they'd seen. They said it was the best thing since apples.

They came into our cave and stared round,
as if wondering where all the trees had gone.
They asked if we could do it all again, in their
cave, as it would be a shame if their children
missed it. "And we'd take it as a great
favour," they said, "if you'd take dinner with
us."

The second time went even better than the first, although my father saw fit to reprimand one of my sisters. "When did you ever," he said, "see a bee picking its nose? It ruins my performance."

But it was only my father who noticed. Everyone else sat open-mouthed; and when we finished, the cheers and clapping almost brought the cave down.

When we got home, my uncle, who is usually the last person to gloat over his triumphs, couldn't resist saying to my father, "Well! It looks as if clean toe-nails and a bearskin hat, so to speak, really can feed nine hungry mouths!"

He was right. Since that wonderful night, the whole world's been our hunter and our cook. We've performed up and down the land, and always to full caves. Next summer we are to go up north, on tour.

Although we live at the dawn of history, my uncle says, we've been first out of bed to ring up the curtain!

Look out for more enthralling titles in the Storybooks series:

The Saracen Maid by Leon Garfield

Young Gilbert Beckett is captured by pirates and sold to a rich Eastern merchant. While in captivity, he falls in love with the merchant's beautiful daughter . . .

Fair's Fair by Leon Garfield

It's a week before Christmas, and Jackson is frozen and starving. But one kind act by the street urchin leads to unexpected rewards.

Princess by Mistake by Penelope Lively

What would you do if, one ordinary afternoon, your sister were suddenly kidnapped by a knight and carried away to a castle?

The Midnight Moropus by Joan Aiken

At midnight, on the eve of his birthday, Jon waits at the waterfall to see if the ghost of a long-dead moropus will appear.

The King in the Forest by Michael Morpurgo

While a boy, Tod rescues a young fawn from the King's huntsmen. Many years later, Tod finds his loyalty to his old friend the deer put to the test . . .

All these books and many more in the Storybooks series can be purchased from your local bookseller. For more information about Storybooks, write to: *The Sales Department, Simon & Schuster Young Books, Campus 400, Maylands Avenue, Hemel Hempstead HP2 7EZ.*